# MR LOOPY
## and Mrs Snoopy

# MR LOOPY
## and Mrs Snoopy

*Stories by*
## Sue Limb

*Illustrated by*
## Keith Brumpton

**ORCHARD
BOOKS**
LONDON

FIRST STORYBOOKS

**Big and Little**
Sue Limb
Pictures by Siobhan Dodds

**Big and Little at Home**
Sue Limb
Pictures by Siobhan Dodds

**Mary, the Witch and
the Ten Little Brothers and Sisters**
Cathy Lesurf
Pictures by John Bendall

Text copyright © Sue Limb 1989
Illustrations copyright © Keith Brumpton 1989
First published in Great Britain by
ORCHARD BOOKS
96 Leonard Street, London EC2A 4RH
*Orchard Books Australia*
14 Mars Road, Lane Cove NSW 2066
1 85213 168 3
Printed in Belgium

# *Contents*

# ONE

# Christmas Eve

Once upon a time there were two houses, side by side, at the edge of a wood. One was a higgledy-piggledy, topsy-turvy sort of house, with hens roosting on the window sills. That was Mr Loopy's house. In his garden, the cabbages grew all anyhow, and Mr Loopy had tied them down with blue ribbon to stop them blowing away.

The house next door was very sensible and neat, with lace curtains at all the windows. The carrots in the garden grew in straight rows, and there were no blue ribbons anywhere to be seen. This was Mrs Snoopy's house.

One day, Mr Loopy looked up from his cabbage patch and gave a great cry.

"Oooh, goodness!" he shrieked. "It's Christmas Eve! I clean forgot! I didn't buy a Christmas tree or any decorations or anything, and now the shops are all closed! Oh help! What shall I do?" He ran round and round the cabbage patch to help him to think.

Behind her lace curtains, Mrs Snoopy was watching. Her long red nose nearly touched the window pane, and as she peeped out, she went on knitting, knitting, all the time.

"Just look at that!" she snapped to her husband, Mr Sidney Snoopy. "He's running round his cabbage patch! Whatever next! My word!" But her husband Mr Sidney Snoopy was fast asleep in his chair.

Outside, Mr Loopy stopped running round the cabbage patch and fell over backwards onto the rhubarb. "I must have a Christmas tree!" he cried. But there was no Christmas tree in his garden: only cabbages and turnips and some rather squashed rhubarb. Then he noticed his old broom made of twigs, a bit like a witch's broom, that he used to sweep up the dead leaves every autumn.

"That's it," he cried. "That'll do! It's not really much like a Christmas tree, but never mind!"

And he picked it up and charged indoors.

"He's taken that dirty old broom indoors!" hissed Mrs Snoopy, her knitting needles clicking faster. "Whatever is he up to?" And she climbed up onto a kitchen chair, so as to be able to see into Mr Loopy's kitchen.

Mr Loopy stuck the broom handle into a big vase, so the twigs were all pointing up into the air. It did look quite like a tree.

"What next?" he said. "Oh yes—the decorations. Oh my goodness! I haven't got any."

So he rushed outdoors and undid all the blue ribbon that he had used to tie his cabbages down.

"Dear me!" he puffed. "I suppose all the cabbages will blow away now! But it can't be helped. I must have some Christmas decorations!" And he ran indoors and draped the blue ribbon all over the Christmas tree. It really did look quite pretty.

"Now what?" thought Mr Loopy. "Oh crumbs—the fairy! There's always a fairy on top of the Christmas tree!" He ran to his back door and made a calling-the-fairies sort of noise: TWEETY TWEETY TWEET TWEET TWEET! But no fairies came. A mangy old cat came instead.

"Hello, cat!" said Mr Loopy. "Would you like to wear a silver skirt, and sit at the top of my Christmas tree?"

"Not quite my style, squire," growled the cat. "I wouldn't mind gettin' a saucer of milk down me neck, though."

"Oh, then come in—come in, do!" said Mr Loopy.

"He's taken that mangy old cat in!" cried Mrs Snoopy. "How disgusting, how dreadful, how dirty!" But Mr Sidney Snoopy was still asleep by the fire.

Mr Loopy gave the cat a saucer of milk. The cat drank it and jumped into the peg basket.

"A peg!" cried Mr Loopy. "Of course!"

He seized a peg, wrapped a little bit of silver paper round it, and stuck it on top of the tree. It really did look quite like a fairy. Mr Loopy was pleased.

After lunch, Mrs Snoopy was peering through her window again. And what she saw nearly made her stop her knitting.

"Look what he's doing now!" she cried. "He's up

there on his roof! With a salt-cellar! Whatever next?" But Mr Sidney Snoopy just snored on.

Outside on the roof, Mr Loopy was trying not to look down. He held on tight to the chimney, and shivered with fright and cold.

"Oh, goodness!" he trembled. "I feel quite dizzy. It's dangerous up here! But I must put some salt on the roof, or Santa's reindeer will slip."

That was it, you see. Mr Loopy was terribly worried because it was Christmas Eve, and he knew that tonight Santa Claus would land on his roof with his reindeer. "And wouldn't it be terrible," thought Mr Loopy with a worried frown, "if they slipped and fell...crashed right off my roof...bits of antlers and bells and things all over the place—and none of the children would get their presents."

He sprinkled salt all over his frosty roof, so that the icy tiles would not be slippery any more.

Then he had another thought. He stared down inside his chimney.

"Oh dear!" he said to himself. "It's a bit small, isn't it? I wonder if Santa will be able to squeeze down it? I mean, he's a bit—a bit on the *plump* side, isn't he? Wouldn't it be terrible if he got stuck in my chimney?" It made Mr Loopy go green just to think about it. He lurched down the ladder, ran indoors and returned with a packet of butter.

"He's buttering the chimney now!" gasped Mrs Snoopy from behind her lace curtains. Her knitting needles were back in action, clicking so fast that sparks flew off them. "Well, I never! How silly can you get?"

But Mr Loopy was pleased with his day's work. His roof was thoroughly salted, so the reindeer wouldn't fall, and his chimney was thickly buttered, so Santa would slip down nicely. Mr Loopy went to bed and hung his stocking up.

Standing on a chair, Mrs Snoopy could just see into Mr Loopy's bedroom, next door.

"Well, blow me down!" she cried. "He's hung his stocking up! Surely he doesn't believe in Santa Claus! How loopy can you get?"

But her husband, Mr Sidney Snoopy, was already in bed, fast asleep. So he just snored and snored. Would Santa come, or not? Only time would tell.

TWO

## Christmas Day

When the sun came up over the wood, and Mrs Snoopy woke up, she didn't say, "Happy Christmas!" to her husband, Mr Sidney Snoopy. Nor did she give him a Christmas present. She just got up, crunched a few cold carrots for her breakfast, and peered out at Mr Loopy's house through the kitchen window. Her mouth fell open, but no sound came out. For once she was lost for words, because guess what she saw?

Mr Loopy's house was full of presents, piled high on the kitchen table, and all done up in beautiful paper: orange, and pink, and red. She could see Mr Loopy opening them. Santa had

visited Mr Loopy in the night, and he was so pleased with the salted roof and the buttered chimney that he had left Mr Loopy some marvellous things.

"Oranges!" shouted Mr Loopy joyfully. "And tangerines ... and nuts ... and a Christmas pudding! And mince pies! ... And a train set! ... And scented soap! ... And a pink track suit! Just what I've always wanted!"

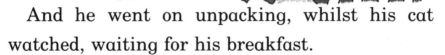

And he went on unpacking, whilst his cat watched, waiting for his breakfast.

Mr Loopy fed the cat. He put the Christmas pudding into a pan to cook, and he crumbled up a few of the mince pies and threw them out for the birds. But then he saw Mrs Snoopy's curtains twitch next door. He knew she was watching him, and he felt a bit sorry for her.

"Poor Mrs Snoopy!" he thought. "I bet she's eating cold carrots as usual. She doesn't believe in Christmas. It must be ever so miserable in her house. No decorations, no presents ... no wonder her nose is so long and red."

He ran indoors, picked up a basket, and filled it with oranges and nuts and scented soap and mince pies. Then he took it next door and rang the Snoopys' bell.

"Oooooh, whatever's that?" cried Mrs Snoopy. "What on earth can he want? Whatever it is, I haven't got it! And if I had, he couldn't have it! What does he mean by ringing my doorbell so early in the morning? Well, whatever he wants, he won't get it!"

And she flew to the door and flung it open.

"No!" she cried. "Not today, thank you!"

"Happy Christmas!" said Mr Loopy, and handed her the basket.

"What's this?" snapped Mrs Snoopy, glaring suspiciously at it.

"It's a Christmas present from me," beamed Mr Loopy. "Good day!"

And he scampered cheerfully back to his own house.

Mrs Snoopy was so surprised, she was downright astonished. Nobody had ever given her a present before. She took the basket indoors and unpacked it, whilst her husband Mr Sidney Snoopy sat in his chair and snored. Mrs Snoopy nibbled one of the nuts.

"Stale!" she said grumpily. "Stale and musty! Horrible!" Then she tried a tangerine. "Oh! It's sour! Much too acid! It'll give me one of my funny stomach attacks, I shouldn't wonder."

All the same, the oranges looked all right, and even Mrs Snoopy had to admit that the scented soap smelt quite pleasant. Mrs Snoopy began to feel almost pleased. She wasn't used to feeling pleased, and it alarmed her a bit. She didn't know quite what to do.

"Oh, what a nuisance!" she thought. "He's given me this present, this basket of bits and pieces. So I suppose I ought to give him a present, too. But it's Christmas Day, and all the shops are shut. What a nuisance! How thoughtless of him!"

She sat by the fire, knitting fiercely, and trying to think of something to give Mr Loopy. It was hard, because everything she thought of, she wanted to keep for herself.

"I suppose I could give him a pair of Sidney's socks," she thought. "But no! Why should I? A lovely pair of socks like that! You can't compare them to a dirty old basket of rotten fruit and nuts. Oh, no!" And she threw another lump of coal on the fire. In the bottom of the coal-scuttle were two tiny lumps of coal, and they gave her an idea.

"Ah!" she thought. "That's what I'll give him!" And she picked them out. Then she went over to her knitting bag, and in the bottom she found a  tangled lump of left-over wool. "Perfect!" said Mrs Snoopy, and darted off to the kitchen. Right at the bottom of the vegetable rack was a woody old carrot. She seized it.

Mrs Snoopy didn't have any pretty wrapping paper, so she bundled the things up in old newspaper. Then she darted across to Mr Loopy's house, rang the doorbell, placed the parcel on the doorstep and dashed back to her own kitchen. What would Mr Loopy think of his present? I wonder . . .

# THREE

# The Snow

**M**r Loopy opened his door and unwrapped the parcel Mrs Snoopy had left him.

"Oh, my goodness!" he said in surprise. "A piece of coal! No, two pieces! How useful! And a carrot! Delicious, I'm sure! And some left-over wool. Well... you never know when it might come in useful. How kind of her to think of me."

Mr Loopy's cat stirred slightly in the peg basket, and waved his tail. His green eyes glowed, and he yawned.

"If you ask me, squire," he growled, "that woman's askin' for her come-uppance."

"Her what?" asked Mr Loopy. "Dear cat, do explain."

"I'll explain it all to you," said the cat with a sly smile. "It's all to do with Mrs Snoopy needin' to be taken down a peg or two."

"Taken down a what?" asked Mr Loopy with a worried frown.

"Come over here," said the cat. "I'll whisper it..."

While the cat was whispering to Mr Loopy, Mrs Snoopy was busy next door, finishing the last of the nuts Mr Loopy had given her.

"Thank goodness those horrible nuts are

finished!" she snapped. "They got behind my teeth something terrible."

Then she stuck her long red nose against the window pane, looking for something else to be angry about.

Outside, lots and lots of big white flakes were whirling down through the air, and settling down in a dazzling carpet on Mr Loopy's cabbages.

"It's snowing!" exclaimed Mrs Snoopy angrily. "Typical! How provoking! Doesn't it make you want to spit!" And she started to knit very fast indeed, glaring out at the snow all the time with her hard little black eyes.

When Mr Loopy next door saw it was snowing, he was delighted.

"Hooray!" he cried. "Come on, cat! Let's go out in the snow, and—well—sort of throw it about a bit."

The cat stayed curled up warm in the peg basket, but Mr Loopy went outside. He hadn't got a warm jumper, so he went out in his shirt-sleeves. But though he felt very cold, he was wonderfully excited.

"How very, well, you know—*beautiful* the snow is!" said Mr Loopy as the snowflakes danced around him. "And how lovely and cold!" Mr Loopy opened his mouth and a few snowflakes landed inside it. They tasted odd: all icy and tickly. "Oh goodness gracious," said Mr Loopy to himself, "maybe I shouldn't eat snow! I mean, well, it might be sort of dirty, you see. I wonder if it is? I wonder if the snow's dirty, or not?"

He looked up to try and decide if it was. When he looked up, against the sky, the snow looked dirty, but when he looked down, on the ground, the snow looked lovely: clean and white.

"I can't decide!" he laughed. "Too hard for me! I think I'll make a snowman instead!"

And he started to make a snowman, next to the fence.

Mrs Snoopy was watching him from behind her lace curtains.

"Oh, look at that!" she said with a scowl. "He's out there, throwing all that snow about all over the place. Making it all so untidy! It's a disgrace, isn't it, Sidney?"

But Mr Sidney Snoopy her husband only snored.

"You'd think he could find something useful to do indoors!" she went on. "He could make use of my lovely presents, for a start. Why doesn't he put those two pieces of coal on the fire? Or make a soup out of that delicious carrot? Or knit himself a hat out of that wool? But oh no—not him. Instead he has to rush about in the snow, like a wild thing. What a nitwit!"

She rattled her knitting needles so hard together that they cracked like fireworks. Outdoors, Mr Loopy was still digging in the snow. Mrs Snoopy watched him, pressing her long red nose to the window pane and peering through the lace curtains with her hard little black eyes.

Then Mrs Snoopy suddenly stopped knitting, and her mouth fell open. She couldn't speak, she was so surprised. Because what do you think she could see out of her window? It was the snowman Mr Loopy had made. Or rather...it wasn't a snowman at all, but a snow-*woman*. Yes!

The snow-woman was peering over the fence, peeping towards Mrs Snoopy's house. There were two little black lumps of coal for eyes—just like Mrs Snoopy's eyes; and a long pointy carrot for the nose—just like her nose; and a tangle of wool for the hair—just like her hair. Mr Loopy had used all the things she'd given him, the coal and the carrot and the wool, to make a snow-woman who looked exactly like her!

All at once her husband Mr Sidney Snoopy woke up. He looked out of the window and saw the snow-woman that Mr Loopy had made, and he burst out laughing.

"Well, I never! It's you, Gert—to the life! The spittin' image of you!" he chortled. "He's given you your come-uppance, and no mistake. That'll take you down a peg or two, I shouldn't wonder."

Mrs Snoopy couldn't say a word. Was she really as angry-looking as that? Were her eyes so black and hard, and was her nose so long and red? She felt ashamed. She drew the curtains across, and didn't peer or peep out at Mr Loopy for a whole week.

Then, one day when the snow had melted but there was a cold wind blowing, and Mr Loopy was out in his garden in his shirtsleeves, busy with his cabbages, she opened her door and called to him.

"Mr Loopy! Er—excuse me! I've got something for you!"

Mr Loopy looked up. He was astonished to see that her eyes were smiling and friendly, and even her nose did not seem quite so long and red and nosey as it had been before. "It's a jumper!" she said, holding out a parcel. "I knitted it for you. I don't like to see you out here, in this freezing wind, getting cold. Here you are!"

"Why—why—thank you very much!" said Mr Loopy, unwrapping the parcel and putting the jumper on. "How very kind! How *extraordinarily* kind of you, to be sure!"

And from that day on, from one Christmas to the next, they were the very best of friends.